# Contents

KT-873-014

# A Remarkable Ear

## Anne Fine

Illustrated by
Roxana de Rond

*With Alex Laing in mind*

First published in 2020 in Great Britain by
Barrington Stoke Ltd
18 Walker Street, Edinburgh, EH3 7LP

www.barringtonstoke.co.uk

Text © 2020 Anne Fine
Illustrations © 2020 Roxana de Rond

A CIP catalogue record for this book is available
from the British Library upon request

ISBN: 978-1-78112-944-9

Printed by Hussar Books, Poland

# Chapter 1
# Hum it again

I'll tell you how it began. (So long ago! I was so young that I can only remember bits of it. Mum says that I was only *four*.)

On Tuesday mornings, Mum says, she always took me to the library. She told me it was so that I could go to Story Time. But when I think about it now, I'm pretty sure it was because we always did a big shop at the supermarket on that morning, and Mum wanted a rest before the long walk home.

The library has good armchairs and good loos.

And good Story Times. I loved to sit on the fluffy carpet with the other kids to hear Alice and Neil read to us. But I never got to choose a few books to take home with me after, like some of the other children. Mum said, "You'll only lose them." Or, "They'll just get torn and dirty." Or, "I have enough to carry without those."

I didn't mind. I didn't really want to carry them all the way home either.

But that day, Mum says, I didn't want to stay till the end of Story Time. Maybe the book that Neil was reading had pictures so tiny I couldn't see them properly. Or maybe I was just bored. But I got off the mat before the end and said to Mum, "Can we go home now?"

Mum said she told me, "Hang on a minute, Will. I'm not quite ready yet." (I expect she was texting.)

She says I wandered off between the bookshelves. She kept an eye on me, and I kept an eye on her, and then Mum put away her phone, picked up the shopping bags and told me, "OK.  I give up.  Let's go."

We'd only just got to the swing doors when this man stepped in front of us and said, "Excuse me."

Mum says she'd never seen him before.  At first she thought he might be about to ask her for money to buy a hot drink or a sandwich.  But he looked too cheerful to be doing that, so she put down her shopping bags and waited to see what he wanted.

The man pointed at me.  "Your boy here," he told her, "has the most amazing gift."

Mum said, "I didn't see him win a prize at Story Time."  She turned to me.  "Have you left it inside?"

"Not that sort of gift," the man said.  "He has the most remarkable ear."  He leaned down to say to me, "Remember that tune you were humming when you came round the bookcase? Well, hum it again."

I'm always getting told off for making too much noise. So Mum said she wasn't at all surprised when I scowled at the man and told him, "It wasn't me. I wasn't humming."

He rolled his eyes. "Oh yes, you were," he said. "And you were humming this." He hummed a little tune. "So go on. Hum it again."

It was a telly advert tune I really liked. He wanted to hear it, and Mum looked as if she didn't mind, so I hummed it again.

"Good," the man said. "And now hum this." He hummed another tune. I didn't know it, but I hummed it anyway.

"Right," he said. "Now try this one. This one is tricky."

He hummed another tune. It didn't sound very tricky to me, though it was much, much longer than the other two.

Anyhow, I hummed it. Easy-peasy.

The man turned back to Mum. "See?" he said again. "A most remarkable ear!"

# Chapter 2

# I'm saying that he's very *musical*

I'm sure I had no idea what the man meant by "a remarkable ear". Was there something wrong with one of mine? I put up my hands to see if they felt the same as usual.

Mum says she laughed and said, "Oh, Will's noisy all right."

"I'm not saying he's *noisy*," the man corrected her. "I'm saying that he's very *musical*."

"Well, he is noisy too," Mum said. "He never stops."

"Never stops what?" the man asked.

Mum was still laughing. "Never stops singing. Never stops humming. Never stops banging spoons on pans."

The man said, "Good!"

Mum sighed. "Who are you, anyway?" she asked him.

"I'm Alex Brand," the man said. "I'm a music teacher." He was still looking at me. He started to clap his hands, over and over, in a choppy sort of rhythm. "Can you do that?"

"Yes," I said, because I could still hear it in my brain.

Mum gave me a little push. "Go on, then," she told me. "The man's asked you to do it. So do it."

Mum said to do it, so I did.

"Excellent," he said. "How about this?"

He clapped his hands over and over again.
This time it was longer and choppier, with soft
bits and loud bits and lots of little gaps. I waited
till I was quite sure he'd finished, then I clapped
it back at him.

"He's very good," the man said to Mum.
"How old is he?"

"He's three," said Mum.

"I'm not three any more," I said. "I had a
*birthday*. Now I'm *four*."

"We won't start till he's five," the man told
Mum.

"Start what?" asked Mum.

"Music lessons, of course," said Alex Brand.
Then he picked up Mum's shopping bags and
carried them for her all the way back to our

house.  Before he left, Mum says, he wrote down our address on a scrap of paper.  Then he bent down to whisper in my ear.

I do remember what he said.  It was, "Keep humming.  Keep humming and singing and banging spoons on pans.  And don't let your mother stop you.  If she tries to, just bite her."

Then he was off in a hurry, around the wheelie bins and down the street.

# Chapter 3
# You again!

Of course I forgot about the man in the library. (I was only *four*.) And I think he must have forgotten about me, because we only met again when I was seven. It was at my primary school. He was standing by the office window near the front door with his back turned.

I went past singing a march we often sang at the end of Assembly.

(I expect I was singing it loudly. Teachers were always telling me to be more quiet in the corridors.)

He swung around. "Well, well," he said. "It's you again!"

I didn't remember him at all, so I just stared.

The office lady smiled. "Do you two know each other?"

"It's Will, isn't it?" he said. "Yes, that was the name. Will."

I was still staring.

"I'm Alex Brand," he reminded me. "We met in the library when you were only four years old but really good at humming."

"He's still really good at humming," said the office lady. "And singing. Very loudly. In the corridors."

"He can go straight on the list," the man said.

That really worried me. Was I in trouble? "What list?"

"For lessons, of course," said Alex Brand. "I *told* your mother I was a music teacher. And you have such a remarkable ear that it would be a sin for you not to learn to play an instrument. In this school, I teach violin. So violin it is."

Mum's always saying that we can't afford things, so I said, "No, thanks."

"Don't 'No, thanks' me," said Alex Brand. "Your mum agreed that I could come back as soon as you were five. I only didn't because I lost the piece of paper with your address on it. Look at how much you've grown! How old are you now?"

"I'm seven," I admitted.

"See?" Alex Brand said. "We've already wasted two whole years. I don't know why your

mother didn't sign you up as soon as the school sent out the forms last month."

I did remember giving a form to Mum. Sometimes she reads them. Sometimes she says she'll read them later. Mostly I never see them again unless it's a free school trip. Then the office lady phones up to nag Mum to sign them and send them back to school so I can go.

Mr Brand didn't seem to care about forms. All he said was, "You listen to me, Will. From now on, I want you in my violin lessons every Tuesday lunch-time, in the hall."

Now I was even more worried. "But I don't have a violin."

"Don't fret about that," the office lady said. (I think she guessed that I was worrying about how much things would cost.) "The school sorts that out. All that you have to do is go to early lunch on Tuesdays, then show up in the hall." She had another thought. "Just stick with Emma," she told me. "Or Leroy. They're both in your class and they're starting violin lessons too."

I was still worried. I hung around till Mr Brand had gone off down the corridor, then asked the office lady, "Is he allowed to do this? Is he allowed to force me to learn to play the violin?"

"I think he's right," she said. "You have a most remarkable ear, and it's all free. Go home and tell your mum you start on Tuesday. What have you got to lose?"

# Chapter 4
# Off pat by Tuesday

As I was going out of school at the end of the day, the office lady called me back. "Will! Hang on a minute. I have something for you."

I waited by her glass window. I really wanted to hurry out to see if Mum was on the way to meet me. Sometimes she was and sometimes she wasn't. (Mostly, she wasn't.)

The office lady slid a piece of paper out to me. "Here," she said. "Mr Brand asked me to give you this. He says you have to have it off pat by Tuesday."

I'd no idea what she meant. "Off pat?"

"Learn it," she told me. "Learn all the names on it."

It was a sheet of paper with a picture of a violin. All over it were little arrows with the names of the bits. I ran to the corner, waving the paper in my hand.

Mum wasn't there. She wasn't even on the way. But I was used to that. Although she always said she'd *try* to come, she didn't manage often. So on the way home I looked at the paper. Each part of the violin looked a bit like its name. The curled bit at the top was called the scroll. The fat bit was the body. The long thin bit above that was the neck. The four strings went across a sort of bridge, and that was called a bridge. The things that looked like pegs were pegs. So it was all quite easy to remember.

There were nine names, and I'd learned most of them before I even got home.

I rushed off to find Mum. She wasn't in the house. I found her in the back yard, chatting over the fence to Surina.

I couldn't wait for them to finish talking. "Mum!" I said, tugging at her jeans. "Mum! I'm going to learn to play the violin!"

She brushed my hand away. "And I'm going to climb Mount Everest," she said, and went back to talking to Surina.

I waited for a while, but they were gossiping about the man on the corner who won't get his fence fixed. It didn't look as if they were going to stop soon, so I gave up and went inside.

My stepdad, Dave, was on the sofa watching telly. I stood in front of him and said, "I'm going to learn to play the violin."

"Oh, yes?" he said. "And I'm going to play wing back for Man City."

"It's true!" I said. "I am!"

I tried to show him the piece of paper I'd been given, but he pushed me away. "You're blocking the telly, Will."

I went upstairs. My half-sister, Melanie, was getting ready to go off to work.

"I'm going to learn to play the violin," I told her.

"It can't be worse than you humming and singing all the time," was all she said.

I went into my own room. There wasn't much to do, so I just learned the last words on the paper and counted up the days till Tuesday.

There were five.

# Chapter 5
# Plinks and plunks

On Tuesday, when the buzzer rang, Emma and Leroy rushed over to fetch me. "Come on, Will. Early lunch!"

None of the others in the queue were from our year group, so we stuck together. Leroy chose pizza, I had the veggie curry and Emma took a cheese sandwich and a banana out of the lunch box she brings from home.

"Hurry up, Will!" Emma kept saying.

The curry was hotter than usual – both sorts of hot. I did my best to eat it quickly, but in the end I had to leave a lot of it. I wasn't happy about that.  I like to have a lot of lunch at school because by the time Dave or Melanie go up the chippie to get our supper I'm often halfway to starving.

But none of us wanted to be late, so off we went.

Mr Brand was already waiting in the hall. There were seven of us all together – the three of us and four from the other class.  Everyone was given a violin.  Mine came in a bright blue case, and when I lifted up the lid, it looked brand new.  (Well, it was shiny, with no scratches.)

There was a bow clipped in the lid of the case, but Mr Brand told us to leave that alone. He fiddled with the pegs a bit, then told us all to hold our violins as if they were guitars.

He started the lesson.

The time went by in a flash.  We mostly plinked and plunked on the four strings to see how they sounded. It wasn't hard, though it did make my fingertips feel funny. Then Mr Brand gave each of us a small mouth organ thing with only four notes. He called it a tuner and showed us how to turn the pegs until the plinks and plunks sounded the same as the notes on the tuner.

That was the hardest bit of the whole lesson.

Then he played us a tune. He said he made it out of just those four plink plunk notes.

I couldn't believe it when I heard the buzzer go. The lesson had gone past so fast.

"Right," Mr Brand said. "Put away your violins. And don't muck about with them. I want to see them looking just as nice when you bring them back next Tuesday."

When we brought them *back*? Were we allowed to take them *home*?

I watched the others put their violins away and pick up their cases. I watched them hurry out of the hall.

I felt a prod in my back. It was Emma. "Come on!" she told me. "Hurry up!"

I snapped down the lid of my case, checked both the catches and followed her back to our classroom. When we were almost there, she prodded me again. "Ssshh, Will! It's too loud."

Too loud? I didn't even know that I was singing.

# Chapter 6
# Horribly wrong

"You have to practise!" Mr Brand said. "Every single day. You have to practise for at least fifteen minutes." That first week, I don't know how many times I lifted the shiny brown violin out of its case and had a go at getting Mr Brand's plink-plunk tune off pat. I kept forgetting little bits of it and then remembering them again.

"For heaven's sake!" Mum said. "All of that plinking and plunking. You sound like a dripping tap!"

Melanie said, "Are you *supposed* to hold it that way? Like a guitar? I bet you've got that wrong."

Dave said, "You're not starting up again! That's the third time today!"

But I was set on getting that tune right. And by the time Tuesday came round again, I had it off pat. This time, I chose a sandwich for my lunch so I could get all of it eaten before Emma dragged me and Leroy along to the hall.

Mr Brand made us stand in a line. "Right," he said. "Let's hear all of you, one at a time, plucking the strings the way I showed you last week."

He turned to my end of the line.

"You first," he told me.

I looked round at the others. They were all staring at me. It was horrible. I'm not exactly *shy*. I just hate doing things all by myself with other people watching.

But they were waiting. And I was too scared of Mr Brand to ask him to pick someone else to do it first. So I held my violin the way he'd shown us, and I played the plink-plunk tune that I'd been working to get right all week.

When I had finished, I looked round again. Everyone seemed to be staring at me even *more*, and Mr Brand was quiet for a moment. Then he said softly, almost as if to himself, "Oh, I can see this isn't going to work out."

I thought I must have got things horribly wrong.

He moved on to the others. To my surprise, they each just plucked all four of the strings in turn.

Four plinks or plunks. No tune. That's all they did.

I felt like an idiot. I hadn't even got the first thing right. I'd wasted all that time working the tune out, and it wasn't what Mr Brand wanted. My hands went hot and sweaty, which made the rest of the lesson harder when he showed us how to hold the bow and move it across the strings.

As soon as the buzzer rang, we all put our violins back in their cases. Mr Brand gave everyone except for me a sheet of paper from his pile. Then he picked up my violin case. "Who is your teacher?" he asked me.

I told him, "Miss Amir."

"I'll have to talk to her," he said.

I thought it was to tell her I wouldn't have to go to early lunch on Tuesdays any more, as he could see things weren't going to work out.

We went to my classroom, and Miss Amir took him into the quiet corner. I kept my head down, but I saw them looking at me. I felt *terrible*. I knew when I went home without the violin, Mum and Dave and Melanie would say they'd always known it wasn't going to work, and I'd spent the whole week driving them mad, plinking and plunking for nothing.

Then Miss Amir led Mr Brand across to the lesson timetable on the wall. I heard her say firmly, "No. Will *can't* miss spelling. So if he *must* have lessons on his own, he'll have to come to you in morning break."

Mr Brand sighed. "That means I'll have to get here so much earlier."

"I'm sorry," said Miss Amir. "But Will's spelling isn't up to scratch, so he can't miss our Tuesday lesson."

"Morning break it is, then," said Mr Brand. He came across and gave me back my violin and one of the sheets of paper he'd given everyone else. It had a picture of a violin bow, with the names of the parts.

He tapped it with his finger. "By Tuesday morning break," he told me. "Off pat."

I went home singing the names. "The tip ... the stick ... the grip ... the frog (yes, really, that's the black lump at the hand end) ... the hair ... the screw."

I expect everyone who passed me thought that I had gone crazy.

# Chapter 7
# Dead tricky

Problem.

It's not so easy to practise in a house like ours. Dave was always the first to complain. "Will! Turn it down, can't you? I can't hear the telly!"

Melanie was the next to moan. "Will you be going on much longer? You sound like a drowning cat!"

Even Mum used to have a go at me. "Will! Don't play that thing down here! Take it upstairs!"

I wasn't all that happy either. I found practising really annoying. Somewhere in my head I could hear what I was trying to play, but it never came out right. I'd put my fingers in what I thought was the exact right place, but the note would sound wrong. I'd try to draw the bow across one string the way that I'd been shown, but it would scrape against one of the other strings as well as the one I wanted and ruin everything.

It was dead tricky.

Each Tuesday now I had my lessons on my own with Mr Brand at morning break. I'd get all tense and nervy. "Sorry!" I kept on saying. "Sorry!" What came out never sounded like the music playing in my head. It never sounded how I wanted it to sound at all.

I'd tell Mr Brand, "I can't do it!"

"Nonsense," he'd say. "You can't expect to get everything right straight away. Try it again."

So I'd try it again. Over and over.

One Tuesday morning, I got so angry with myself that I burst into tears. I couldn't help it. I was so frustrated. I was *furious*.

Mr Brand didn't say a thing. He took my violin and bow from me and put them in the case. We went back to the classroom together. I kept my head down so the others couldn't see my red face and went back to my seat. Mr Brand had a quiet word with Miss Amir. She nodded, and after he'd gone she said to me, "It's early lunch for you, Will. Mr Brand wants you to go along with Leroy and Emma today."

*So that's that*, I thought. *My special lessons on my own are over. He's put me back with the others. Leroy says he never practises, and Emma told me she's so bad at violin that next*

34

*term she's choosing dance instead. I must be rubbish too.*

Lunch was spaghetti, but I didn't feel like eating much. When we got to the hall, Mr Brand sat me down behind the others and slid my violin case under my chair. "You sit there nice and still and enjoy the concert," he said, and winked.

I could have cried again. He didn't even think that I was good enough to play with the others! I would have run out of the hall, except that my note for the school trip to Manley Rock Pools was in my violin case, and I needed that.

So I sat there, dead miserable, and listened.

And they were terrible! Terrible! Even I could tell that none of them had practised nearly as much as me. Their fingers slid all over the place. Their bows scraped and scratched. They couldn't keep in time. You would have thought they were all playing different tunes.

Then Mr Brand winked at me again over their heads.

And I felt better.

No.  Much more than that.  I felt so happy. I felt *wonderful*.

# Chapter 8
## Up to scratch

The weeks went by. I learned to read music. The tiny black notes that looked like people crowded in a messy bus line turned into music in my head. I got better at bringing my fingers down in the exact right place to make the sound I wanted.

I learned the fancy words. *Lente* meant "play it slowly". *Forte* meant "make it loud and strong". *Andante* meant "go at a steady walking pace".

By half term, Mr Brand was grumbling to Miss Amir again. "Why do I have to come in so early to teach Will? Why can't he just miss spelling?"

"I *told* you," Miss Amir explained. "His spelling isn't up to scratch."

Mr Brand turned to me. "Did you hear what she said? I have to get here by break time to teach you, then hang around for over an hour, doing nothing, before I can teach the others. And all because you're rubbish at spelling."

I saw Miss Amir wince. "I didn't say he was *rubbish*," she said quickly. "I said his spelling wasn't up to scratch."

Mr Brand turned to me. "Well, then," he said. "I'm giving you three weeks to get your spelling up to scratch."

After he'd gone, Miss Amir took me aside. "Who tests you on your spelling words at home?"

"No one," I said.  "I try to do them by myself."

Miss Amir said, "Maybe you'd like me to write a note to your mother?"

"No, don't," I said.  "Let me try to be firm with her first."

"All right," she said.  "But you be *very* firm. And make sure you keep her to it."

So I took my ten words home each day and I was *very* firm.  "I have to get all of them right. Every morning.  For three whole weeks.  And you have to test me."

I could see she knew that I meant it.  And she did try.  Sometimes it was hard to get her to stop what she was doing and listen to me spelling out the words.  And sometimes she didn't even try to do it properly.  Once I'd got nine of them right already, so we were on the last one.  She looked at the list again. "*Mattress.*"

"M – A – T," I began, and then I saw her staring out of the window at Surina, who was waving to her over the fence.

"Q – V – X – T," I finished up.

She handed me the list. "Well done! Finished!"

"Mu-um! That is *not* how you spell mattress! You have to do this *properly*. Surina has to *wait*."

I needed Mum to know that getting all my spellings right was now *important*. So in the mornings I made her test me on all ten of them a second time before I would even pick up my spoon to start on my cornflakes. And I got better and better. At the end of the three weeks Miss Amir told me, in front of everyone, "OK, Will. Only one word wrong yesterday. If you can spell that word correctly now, I'm going to let Mr Brand give you your lessons at the time he wants."

The word was *favourite.* I got it wrong because I was so nervous. But then Miss Amir smiled and said she'd let me miss the spelling lessons anyway, so long as I kept doing my ten words each night.

# Chapter 9
# Did I forget to tell you?

And so the months went past.  And then the years.  I had to hand back the violin I'd been given because it was too small for me now, and Mr Brand gave me another.

Then came the time to change school.

"Where are you going to go?" asked Mr Brand.

I told him.  "Tanner High."

"I don't teach there," he said.  "You'll have to come to my house after school.  If we make it Thursdays, then you can come to me straight after orchestra."

I stared at him. "Orchestra?"

"Did I forget to tell you? I've signed you up for Junior Orchestra. Be at the hall behind the library at half past four."

I *loved* the orchestra. We played all sorts of things. Old, modern, quiet, noisy. Music with drums to make you halfway to deaf. Music to set your feet tapping. Music to make you think of people weeping. Some of the others were older than me, and one or two of them were younger. They played all sorts of things. Flutes. Clarinets. Cellos. Trumpets. Violas.

I sat with a boy called Aleksy. His family had come from Poland, and he had to catch two buses to get to orchestra by half past four. I felt quite lucky, knowing that when term began I'd only have to carry my violin the short way from Tanner High.

Still, as the summer went on, I did get nervous. Tanner High! I'd heard the scary stories. I'd seen the big kids hanging around the streets.

My mum said, "You'll be fine."

Dave said, "After one week, you'll feel as if you've been there for years."

"Just don't let anyone near your violin," warned Melanie.

It was the best advice. On Thursdays, I hid the case in Melanie's old sports bag and slid it way back underneath the shoe rack in the cloakroom. Nobody noticed it there.

My lessons after orchestra were in Mr Brand's front room. I loved the house. It was *enormous* and the most amazing *mess*. There were two massive pianos, one upstairs and one downstairs. Books and sheet music lay not just on the shelves but all over. He kept a heap of violins under the downstairs piano. Under the window was a laundry basket full of spare violin bows.

Even the bathroom halfway up the stairs was knee-deep in sheets of music. Mr Brand's wife was called Miss Miranda, and she taught singing. The upstairs piano was for her, and sometimes when I came to the house I'd see the people who had lessons with her coming down the stairs.  One day when I was leaving I heard one of her students getting to the end of a song. It sounded perfect to me, but after it finished I heard Miss Miranda say, "Never mind, Suzi! We'll get it off pat in the end."

That made me smile, because I got that all the time from Mr Brand: "We'll get it off pat in the end."

# Chapter 10

# Hundreds and thousands
# of hours

As the months went by, I found I had to practise for longer. If I moaned, Mr Brand said, "How do you think that people get good at anything? How many hundreds and thousands of hours do you suppose a world-class footballer has to practise before he can take a penalty and be as sure as he can be that he'll get it right?"

I said, "But everyone at home gets so fed up. They're not nasty. They don't try to stop me. But I know they all hope I'll get bored with the violin and start doing something different. Something *quiet*."

He looked at me as if I were talking Greek.

"I mean it," I said. "My stepdad has to stop himself from saying, 'Oh, not again!', and he turns up the sound on the telly. Mum asks me, 'Will you be going on for very long?' And Melanie comes in my room shouting, 'Will, why can't you play the *tune*? Why just practise tiny bits of it over and over and over?'"

"Right, then," said Mr Brand. "You'll have to practise at school."

"You have to be *joking*!" I told him. "I'm not in primary school any more. If I take out the violin at Tanner High, everyone will want a go. Then someone will start a footie game on the other side of the changing rooms. It wouldn't be *safe*."

(I didn't bother to add, "And nor would I.")

Mr Brand sighed. "No one can practise the violin while the telly is on," he told me. "I'll sort something out."

He did, too. He went to see my head teacher, and she agreed that I could practise every break and lunch-time in the store room behind the kitchens.

I liked that. It was small and warm, and only the cooks could hear me. They were so nice. They always kept me something good to eat. As soon as the bell rang at the end of lunch break, I'd gobble up whatever it was, and when I gave back the plate, they'd say something friendly.

"How *do* you remember all those different scales?"

"That tune was lovely, Will."

"You get better and better."

The only other people who knew where I went in breaks and lunch-times were my best mates, Tom and Arif.

Arif said, "You practise so hard that you should put your name down for the end-of-term Talent Show."

"You might even win," said Tom.

I felt a shiver go down my spine. "I'd never dare play in the Talent Show!" I said.

I never minded playing for Mr Brand. Or with the others in the orchestra. And in the store room, I even used to pretend that all the scarlet floor mops leaning against the wall were a small audience of people with stringy red hair.

But I was sure that I could never play all by myself in front of a hall full of people.

The only other person who knew about the violin hidden in my sports bag was Suzi.

We weren't exactly friends, because she was much older. But every time I saw her after her singing lesson with Miss Miranda, she smiled at me. And every time she saw me carrying the sports bag down the corridor, she gave me a wink.

One day I dared to tell her, "It's easy for you. You can carry your voice around without anyone noticing." And after that, each time I bumped into her, she would pretend to root for something in her bag. "Just checking that I have my voice."

*

Now, bit by bit, my lessons changed. Mr Brand no longer tried to cheer me up all the time. He stopped saying things like, "Don't worry. It'll come" and "You'll soon have it off pat". Instead, he said things like, "Tricky, that bit." Or, "That's going to take some work."

And then, one day, he gave me the *Notebook of Pain and Doom*.

# Chapter 11
# Well, thanks a bunch!

That's what he called it. Honestly! He'd even written that on the first page in huge letters underneath my name:

**The Notebook of Pain and Doom**

"What's that about?" I asked him.

"It's your practice notes," he told me. "I write my advice in it."

"Advice?"

"Yes. My advice. What you must work on at home in the week in order to play better."

I couldn't help it. It popped out. "But I thought I was doing pretty well."

"You are," he said. "Very well. Which is why I expect better." He thought for a moment, then added, "Not just better. Much, *much* better."

*Well, thanks a bunch!* I thought. But I said nothing. While I was playing, I just looked his way now and again and saw him scribble like mad in the new notebook.

As soon as the lesson ended, he handed it over. I left the house and went round the corner before I stopped to see what he'd written.

Suzi was coming along the street after her own lesson upstairs with Miss Miranda. She stopped when she saw me. "Is that one of Mr Brand's Notebooks of Pain and Doom? Can I see? I've heard they're very funny."

"Funny?"

I opened it.  Together we stared.  While I'd been running through my scales for him, he'd clearly been writing: "*Scale of B minor – pretty rubbish.  Scale of A major –* worse," and drawn a picture of a matchstick boy hurling himself, head first, into a rubbish bin.

While I was playing "Spring Song" (which I had worked on for *hours*), he'd written: "*Spring Song – why not try keeping to* time?" and drawn a picture of a cuckoo clock exploding to send cogs and wheels and broken springs flying all over.

While I was playing the hardest piece of all, called "All Alone", Mr Brand had spent the time drawing me as a matchstick boy playing the violin on one side of a desert island.  On the other side, a castaway was sitting with his back to me.  He had his fingers in his ears, and he was saying, "*All Alone?  I wish!*"

"That's nice," I said. "Oh, that is really nice."

Suzi just grinned. "You have to take it as a compliment," she said. "Miss Miranda says he only bothers to give Notebooks of Pain and Doom to his very best pupils."

That made me feel a bit better. But not much.

# Chapter 12
# Please stop before I *kill* you

So that's how we went on.  Each week I went for my lesson after orchestra.  Each week he wrote a lot of advice in the notebook, along with his rude cartoons.  A lady stuffing cotton wool balls into her ears as I opened my case to take out my violin.  Strong men throwing themselves off cliffs in despair because I was playing so badly.  Cats throwing up in their baskets while they were listening to me.

I warned him, "You wouldn't get away with this if you were teaching me in school."

"And you wouldn't get better so fast."

"You could be nice and *polite*."

He stared at me. "Why would I do that? *Why?*"

I couldn't think of any reason, so I just started playing again, and he went back to writing in my notebook.

When I came out, Suzi was still singing in the room upstairs. It was a really lovely song, but it had lots of tricky bits, and she had to stop several times to try it over again.

I waited for her on the wall along the street, reading the notes that Mr Brand had given me. When she came past, I was admiring the very fine cartoon of him using a spare violin bow to stab himself as I was playing.

Suzi stopped to take a look. "Charming," she told me. "Very encouraging."

"I wonder if the teachers know about these notebooks."

Suzi looked puzzled. "Why would your teachers care?"

"Well, the school's paying for our lessons."

"Not mine," said Suzi. "My mother pays for mine."

When I got home, I asked Mum, "Are you paying for my violin lessons?"

"Not me," she said. "Where would I find the money? I thought that they were free, like back in primary."

I wasn't so sure. Next lesson, I asked Mr Brand, "Who's paying for my lessons?"

"No one," he said. "I give them to you free because you have the most remarkable ear."

And that's what he drew in the notebook
that week. The most remarkable ear. That's all.
No notes on the music. No orders. No advice.
Just this weird, curly, mad, huge ear.

I didn't know what to think. But I had to
work even harder now to get the pieces perfect,
so I practised at home again as well as at school.

"Please!" Melanie would yell. "Please stop before I *kill* you!"

"I'll help you hide his body," said my stepdad.

"It has been *hours*, Will," Mum would say, as nicely as she could.

Even Surina from next door said, "We hear you playing every night now. Are you getting ready for the end-of-term Talent Show?"

And then, one morning, I bumped into Miss Amir from my primary school. "Will!" she said. "How nice to see you! I hear you're doing really well."

That startled me. Who would have guessed that teachers talk about you after you've left their school? I asked, "Who told you that?"

She said, "Mr Brand, of course. He still gives violin lessons at our school. He says you're doing so well he thinks you'll get a place at music school."

I knew that Suzi hoped to go to music school. So I thought that maybe something Mr Brand had said about that had got all mixed up and Miss Amir had misunderstood. But it was obvious that Miss Amir was being nice, so I just smiled.

Still, it did set me thinking. And after my next lesson, I waited on the wall for Suzi. She took longer to come out than usual.

She saw me and said, "You must have been here quite a time."

"I wanted to ask you something."

Most people in Suzi's year group wouldn't stop to talk to someone as young as me. They'd just walk past. But Suzi's not like that. She sat on the wall right next to me and said, "I'm sorry

I was so late out. I couldn't get the last song right."

"Is that the tricky one?" To show her which I meant, I hummed the bit where the piano Miss Miranda's playing goes off one way, but Suzi's voice has to soar over it like a bird.

She looked surprised. "Yes, that's the one. I didn't know you could hear us."

"Only when I'm in the hall and putting on my jacket."

She sighed. "I really have to get it right by Tuesday afternoon. That's when I have my test to see if I can try out for a place in music school."

"That's what I wanted to ask you," I told her. "What's music school like?"

She told me everything she knew. It sounded like a lot of work. But making music all day? That would be wonderful!

I had another question, "But what about afterwards?"

"Afterwards?"

"After you leave," I said. "What sort of job would you get then?"

Her face went a little dreamy. "Well, if I was really good, I suppose I'd get to sing more and more."

"Like in a chorus or a choir?"

"Maybe," she said. "Or even solo." She saw my puzzled face. "You know," she said. "In concerts and recitals. Or opera."

"What, singing all by yourself? On stage in front of everyone? Like in the Talent Show?"

That same old shudder ran down my spine. Just the idea of being the only one making the music in a hall full of strangers made me feel *terrified*. Suppose you didn't get the notes off pat? People would *notice*.

But I was thinking something else as well. If Suzi was hoping to go off to music school from Tanner High, that meant that all of the people I'd ever heard singing on radio or television could possibly have started off making their music in a normal school.

Like Suzi.

And like me.

# Chapter 13
# A million miles high

On Monday morning, the poster was up on the notice board:

**TANNER HIGH'S GOT TALENT**
**End-of-term concert**
**Sign up now**

Tom pointed. "You ought to enter. My mum says that you're very good." (His mum's a dinner lady.)

"Yes," said Arif. "You might even win a prize."

"No way!" I said. "Forget it!"

"You can't keep that violin a secret all your life!" Arif told me firmly. And sure enough, the very next day, after lunch, almost as soon as we were back in class, in came Mr Henry. I heard him say to Mrs Snow, "Do you have a boy called Will in here? Good at the violin?"

I couldn't put my head down fast enough.

Mrs Snow didn't sound sure. "We have a Will," she said. "I know he's always carrying a sports bag down the corridor. But I don't know about him being musical." Raising her voice, she asked me, "Will, do you play the violin?"

Everyone stared. I gave a shrug as if to say, "Sorry. I don't know what you're talking about."

Mr Henry shook his head sadly. "That's a shame. This was the last class to check. I'll have to go back and tell Suzi Tang there has been some mistake."

Suzi?

Tuesday! Her big test for the chance to go to music school!

"I think she *might* mean me," I mumbled.

Mrs Snow looked at me again. "Come on, Will. Do you play the violin? Or don't you?"

Emma, two seats away, said, "He did play back in primary school."

Arif said, "He still does."

Tom pitched in as well. "He's good, too. My mum often hears him practising."

I stumbled to my feet. "Yes," I admitted. "Suzi means me."

"Well, hurry up!" said Mr Henry. "Go fetch your violin and meet us in the hall. Right now!"

Suzi was already there, looking all red and panicky. "Will! Miss Day here has to finish my test right now. She has two other people to hear this afternoon. And I've been stupid and left the music for that tricky song at home!"

Miss Day said to Suzi, "Why not sing something else?"

But Suzi was almost in tears. "No!" she said. "This is my very best piece – the one I want you to hear." She turned to me. "You'll play it, won't you, Will? I know you know it."

I looked round. There was Mr Henry, watching us. And this Miss Day. And three of the dinner ladies, standing there holding their mops.

Almost an audience. I couldn't do it!

But how could I let Suzi down? She'd always been so nice to me. And Miss Day would be listening to her, not to me. I knew Mr Henry would just be glad he'd helped to sort out the problem. The dinner ladies heard me almost every day. And I'd played for those bright red mops a thousand times before.

"All right," I said to Suzi. "I'll give it a go."

Suzi was so delighted, she almost hugged me.

And so I played. The moment I began, I realised how often I had heard the song while I was laying my violin back in its case, or clipping my bow in the lid, or putting on my jacket. I pretty well knew it backwards.

We made a lovely job of it. As soon as we started, Suzi's confidence came back. Her voice rang round the hall. Miss Day was smiling at her all the time.

"Well done!" she said to Suzi as soon as we'd finished. "You sang that beautifully." She turned to me. "And you? You had it off pat.

A most remarkable ear. I'm sure that in no time at all I shall be back to test *you*."

I stared. Did she mean I could get to music school one day as well? I was sure she did. I felt a million miles high.

So high that when Mr Henry said, "Right, then. You two must definitely enter the Talent

Show!", I didn't even worry about what everyone would think.

I just looked forward to it.

# Chapter 14
# Stars of the show

I took the news home.

Mum said, "I *told* that Mr Brand right at the start that you had a remarkable ear."

Dave said, "I always kept the house dead quiet while you were practising."

"I'm so glad I encouraged you to keep on playing," said Melanie.

I stared at the three of them. But before I could even begin to put them right, I saw that Mum was rooting in her purse. "How much are the tickets?  Because we wouldn't miss this for the world."

"No," Melanie agreed.  "We'll be right there, in the front row, cheering you on."

Dave said, "I reckon you and Suzi Tang will be the Stars of the Show."

*

So here we are – me and Suzi Tang, side by side on the stage.  Suzi's family and mine are in the front row, next to Mr Brand and Miss Miranda. Everyone's clapping and cheering.  Some people from my class are stamping their feet and whooping, and no one is trying to stop them. Miss Amir and Mr Henry are smiling like crazy. Some of the dinner ladies are waving, and Tom and Arif have all four thumbs up.

Suzi takes hold of my free hand and leads the two of us right to the front of the stage.  We take one bow and then another.  And another.

The cheering goes on and on. I look down at the front row and see that Mr Brand is drawing a huge ear in the air on the side of his head, and grinning at me. I nearly burst out laughing.

Then Suzi turns to me and says, "We *did* it, Will!"

"Off pat!" I agree.

We take another bow. (I suppose I'll have to practise those as well, if I'm to go to music school. And I most definitely am!)

Our books are tested
for children and young people by
children and young people.

Thanks to everyone who consulted on
a manuscript for their time and effort in
helping us to make our books better
for our readers.